Julian's Glorious Summer

By Ann Cameron
Illustrated by Dora Leder

HARCOURT BRACE & COMPANY

Orlando   Atlanta   Austin   Boston   San Francisco   Chicago   Dallas   New York
Toronto   London

To Karen Herman,
who told me work is nice—
especially when it's done

A.C.

This edition is published by special arrangement with Random House, Inc.

Grateful acknowledgment is made to Random House, Inc. for permission to reprint *Julian's Glorious Summer* by Ann Cameron, illustrated by Dora Leder. Text copyright © 1987 by Ann Cameron; illustrations copyright © 1987 by Dora Leder.

Printed in the United States of America

ISBN 0-15-307539-2

8 9 10 025 99

Contents

1.

Why I Tell Stories

I am a nice person. I practically almost always tell the truth. I really don't like making up stories. I only do it when absolutely necessary. That's the way it was at the beginning of the summer.

It was the first morning after school got out. I was sitting in our swing, making circles in the sand with my tennis shoe and watching some ants go by. Every last one was in a hurry.

"Take your time!" I said to them. "This is vacation!"

But they went on running as fast as they

could. They acted like they were all late.

"Where are you going so fast?" I asked.

I wasn't in a hurry. I was happy. My little brother, Huey, was with my dad at his car repair shop. My mother was at her job. I was waiting for my best friend, Gloria. I was thinking how much fun Gloria and I (and Huey, when I let him play with us) would have all summer.

I was thinking so much, I hardly looked at the street. I almost didn't see a girl on a blue bicycle going by fast—and when I did, I thought, "That can't be Gloria!" because Gloria doesn't have a bicycle.

The girl on the blue bicycle didn't stop. She didn't even look at me.

That was a relief. It couldn't be Gloria.

And then the girl came by once more, a little slower. She had braids just like Gloria's, flying flat out behind her in the breeze.

Still she didn't look at me or stop. So I thought to myself, "It *can't* be Gloria."

But I was worried. I said to myself, "What if it *is* Gloria? What if it's Gloria's bike?"

I decided to go into action.

I got out of the swing. I stood with my feet as close together as possible, my hands rolled into fists, and my eyes shut tight.

I kept my eyes shut for a long time, concentrating.

On the blackness inside my eyelids, I pictured the blue bicycle.

Then I made my wish, very slowly, out loud, three times.

"Let it not be Gloria's.

"Let it NOT be Gloria's.

"Let it not be GLORIA'S," I said.

The air, the trees, and the sky were all stamped with my wish.

I opened my eyes.

A face was one inch from my face.

It was Gloria's.

She said, "Did anybody call my name?"

The world came into focus. Behind Gloria, on the grass, I saw a blue bicycle.

I unrolled my fists.

I moved my feet apart.

"Your name?" I said to Gloria.

"Yes, Julian," Gloria said. "My name. Also, I think I should tell you, about thirty thousand ants are crawling up the back of your pants."

I looked behind me. Sure enough, Gloria was right. I moved away from the ant trail and brushed the ants off my pants.

"I thought I heard my name," Gloria said again. "I thought I heard you say something really strange. I thought I heard you say 'Let it not be Gloria's.' "

"Oh, *that,*" I said. "I was making a wish."

"But weren't you saying my name?" Gloria persisted.

I was embarrassed. "Of course not," I said. "Of course I wasn't saying your name."

"What were you saying, then, Julian?" Gloria asked.

It was one of those times when I didn't want to tell the truth. And just like magic, it came to me—what I could make up.

2.

I Get Out of Trouble

"It didn't have anything to do with you," I said. "I was wishing for a glorious summer. I said, 'Let it not be glorious.' It was a reverse boomerang wish. You wish backwards. You say the opposite of what you want. Then what you really want will come sneaking up from behind you."

" 'Let it not be glorious'?" Gloria said.

"That's right," I said. "That was my reverse wish."

"Well, I hope it works," Gloria said. "I mean, I hope it comes out backwards, the way you want it to.

"Anyhow," she said, "it's too bad you had your

eyes closed when I came up. I wish you'd seen me! I just rode that bicycle right up here on the grass!"

"Oh," I said, "you borrowed a bicycle?"

I was hoping there was still some power in my wish.

Gloria smiled a huge smile. "It's not borrowed!" she said. "It's mine!"

My wish was dead. Maybe it had stamped the sky, the trees, and the air. But it hadn't touched the blue bicycle.

"Just like that, you got a bicycle?" I said.

"Yes! My mom and dad got it for me yesterday!" Gloria hopped and did a little zigzag dance, the way she does when she's happy.

"So," I said, "in a couple years, when you know how to really ride it, you're going to ride it a lot?"

"Julian!" Gloria said. She knocked her braids back behind her head, the way she does when she gets serious. "I can ride it right now! You should have seen me! I rode up to your house three times. The first time, I was going to wave. But I was scared that if I waved, I would fall over. The second time, I was going to turn into your driveway. But I couldn't make the turn. The third time, it was easy!"

"Great," I said, as if it wasn't really so great.

"Yes! I can ride a bike!" Gloria said. "My mom and dad taught me last night. Aren't you going to congratulate me, Julian?"

"Oh, sure, congratulations," I said.

"You don't sound very enthusiastic, Julian," Gloria said.

"But wait till you see mine!" Gloria said. She ran over to the bicycle on the grass and stood it up. It had fat tires and a bell, a silver arrow on the front, and red plastic streamers coming out of the handlebars. It was nice—if you like bicycles.

"See, Julian!" Gloria said. She rang the bell.

"I can teach you to ride," she said.

"Thanks, but no thanks," I said.

"You don't want to learn?"

I wished Gloria could talk about something else besides stupid bicycles for a change.

"So," Gloria said. "Answer me! Don't you want to learn?"

"No, I don't want to learn," I said.

"Well, okay, then. See you sometime. Good-bye," Gloria said.

The way she said good-bye didn't sound usual. It sounded permanent.

She turned her bicycle around and started pushing it out to the street.

I got the opinion I might be losing my best friend.

"Gloria! Wait a minute! Stop!" I shouted.

Gloria stopped, but she didn't turn around.

I ran in front of her.

She looked as if she was crying. But I must have been wrong, because Gloria never cries.

"So?" Gloria said.

"Gloria," I said, "listen! It's just—" I thought

of telling the truth: my opinion about bicycles. But if I did that, Gloria might think I was afraid of bicycles, which is not the truth at all. I am not afraid of lions. I am not afraid of tigers or dinosaurs. So how could I be afraid of a little thing like a bicycle?

Just so Gloria wouldn't get the wrong idea, I made something up.

"It's just that there's a lot to do around the house," I said. "My dad has decided to make me work very hard all summer. So I won't have time to learn to ride a bicycle. That's all."

"Oh!" Gloria said. Her smile came out all sudden and shining, like a rainbow after a storm. "I didn't know that!"

I could see that we were friends again. I could see that Gloria felt sorry for me.

"You won't have any time off?" Gloria asked.

I wondered what to say, yes or no. If I said I would have time off, then there would be time to learn to ride a bicycle. The best answer was no.

"I'll be working practically night and day," I said. I tried to sound brave, as if I could take all the jobs Dad could give me and not complain.

"I was working all morning," I added. "I have to work again pretty soon."

Gloria looked at my house. Her eyes got big— as if she was looking at a prison.

"Well, anytime you don't have to work, you know you are always welcome to visit me," she said.

"Thank you," I said. I tried to sound braver than ever, like a spaceboy who had to be left behind on an asteroid.

Gloria sighed. She put her hand on my shoulder.

"See you later," she said. "Try to be happy."

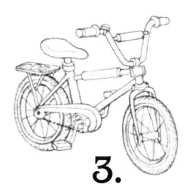

3.

My Father Talks to Heaven

After Gloria left I decided to actually do some work.

I went upstairs to check on my rock collection. Before breakfast I found out Huey had been stealing my sharp rocks and storing them under my mattress. I decided to see that they were in the right place—under Huey's mattress. They were—and their points were still as sharp as the peaks of the Rocky Mountains.

I made my bed. Then I made Huey's bed and fluffed up the pillows. If my mother thanked me for making Huey's bed, I would say, "Oh, I'm sure he'd do the same for me!"

With that work done, I went and sat on the porch. I thought it was still a very good summer—even though it would be a much better summer if Gloria had never gotten a bicycle. And I was glad that Gloria felt sorry for me. If I went over to her house, she would probably even stop riding her bicycle to play with me. If she wanted me to learn to ride, I could always say I had a job to do at home and leave. I was glad I was smart and had gotten myself out of trouble with Gloria in a quick, simple way.

I smiled and stretched my legs out and looked up through the leaves of the trees in the front yard.

I was pretending I was a fish swimming in the sky when I heard my dad's truck turn into the driveway.

I stood up and shook off my fish scales.

Huey and Dad got out of the truck.

"Hi, Julian," Huey said. He sounded very sweet—as if he was not the person who had moved my collection of sharp rocks from my shelf and put them under my mattress. But I knew he was.

"Hi, Huey!" I said. I gave him a fish-fanged smile.

"HEL-lo, Julian!" my dad said in a super-friendly voice.

Usually that voice means trouble. I checked my dad's eyes. Sure enough, little red and blue flames were leaping in them, like in a furnace that would melt steel.

But I stayed cool. "Hi, Dad," I said. Whatever he had that look in his eyes for, it couldn't be because of me.

"Guess who we just met in the road, Julian!" Huey said. "Gloria! Does she ever have a great bicycle!"

My life was getting worse all the time. Now Huey liked bicycles.

"It's okay," I said. "If you like bicycles."

"We saw it up close," my father said. "Very close."

He gave me an extra-big steel-bending smile.

"Gloria waved to us—I thought her bike was going to fall over — and then I stopped the truck on the side of the road. It looked like Gloria was going to ride her bike straight in my window. But she didn't."

"She didn't," I repeated.

"She didn't. But I thought to myself, 'Gloria

must be in a mighty big hurry to tell me something.' And I was right."

"You were right," I repeated.

I felt the way I feel during a horror movie when I don't like how the story is going and I want to leave.

Only this wasn't a movie.

I couldn't leave.

"And you know what GLORIA told me?" my father said, spreading his hands wide in the air as he said her name—as if it was a pretty rug he was shaking over the whole sky.

"What Gloria told you?" I said.

"Yes. What Glooooooooria toooooooold me," my father repeated. He threw his hands high in the air again and raised his eyes to the sky, as if he wanted to make sure heaven was listening.

"I don't know," I said. I tried to make my voice come out big, or at least normal size. But it came out very little.

"Glooooooooooria toooooooooold me," my father began, "she toooooooooold me that it is a shame that I am making you work practically night and day, all summer long. She said that it is *terrible* that I am giving you so many jobs that you won't even have time to learn to ride a bicycle. She said that she was very surprised. She said that she didn't think I was that kind of man."

"That kind of man," I said. My words came out all white and thin, like a little skinny piece of spaghetti.

"I am *pretty, pretty* sure," my father said, "that Gloria thinks I am mean, mean, MEAN!"

He raised his eyes to heaven again, as if he was saying: "Now, Lord, don't just *listen* to that one. Mark it *down*!"

I was standing practically under my dad's

chin. It seemed way too close, but still as far away as the moon.

"Now, since I don't remember saying *any*thing to you about working day and night, all summer long, I was very tempted to ask Glooooooooooria *what* she was talking about. But I didn't. I decided to ask you first, Julian."

Suddenly my dad bent his knees and slid down as fast as if he was sliding down an invisible firehouse pole, until he was sitting on his heels and looking up into my face. Tell-the-truth sparks were shooting out of his eyes.

"So now I'm asking, Julian. *What* was Gloria talking about?"

I was afraid I was going to swallow my spaghetti-string voice. I was afraid I'd never talk again.

"Just a minute," I said. "I can explain." And I told my brain to come up with something—fast.

4.

I Get Lucky

"Gloria didn't understand," I said to my dad. "I *did* tell her you had a lot of jobs around the house. But what I meant was, I *want* to work a lot this summer. I want to save money for when I am grown up," I added.

My father got into one of his thinking positions. He spread his feet out. He curled his right hand up in a fist and stuck it between his knees and his chin, like a brace.

"Now, let me try to understand this," he said. "You are seven years old. You want to work practically night and day, all summer long, to save money for when you are grown up?"

"Yes," I said. "I want to save money for a race car."

"Do you know how much a race car costs?"

"Not exactly."

"But you want to work practically night and day, all summer long, to buy one?"

"Definitely," I said.

I guessed what my father would say next. I guessed he would say he didn't have that many jobs for me. In my mind I practiced saying "That's okay, Dad. I don't mind."

My dad said, "Well, Julian, you're in luck! I think I can keep you busy practically all day, all summer long. We'll skip the nights," he said. "Well, what do you say, Julian?"

"Terrible!" I said. "I mean, terribly nice of you! I mean, work—wonderful! What luck!"

I raised my hands to heaven the way Dad does.

Then I collapsed on the grass.

I didn't get up for a long time.

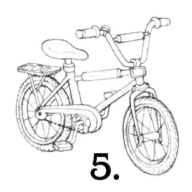

5.

To Each His Own

Right after lunch my dad offered Huey the same great opportunity he'd offered me—to work all summer. "No, thanks," Huey said. "I'd rather go play at Gloria's house." And he left.

"More sharp rocks for you, Huey!" I thought.

But pretty soon there was not even time to think about sharp rocks. My dad gave me my jobs.

To begin with, I polished twelve pairs of shoes, including two pairs my dad had been saving for a dog to chew, if we ever got a dog.

Then I swept the porch.

Afterward I brushed cobwebs off the porch

ceiling and under the eaves all around the house.

When I finished that, it was four o'clock. I sat down. My neck ached from reaching high to get all the spider webs. I pushed my head around with my hands to make sure it still moved as many ways as it used to. I wasn't sure it did.

At four thirty my dad came home from the shop. "Hello, Julian," he called. He came over to check on the work.

"I think we're practically all out of jobs around here," I said.

My dad looked at me. He had little orange sparks in his eyes.

"Don't worry, Julian!" he said. "I'd hate for you to be out of work! There are still plenty of jobs for you!"

And he got me started weeding the garden.

One good thing I noticed about weeding the garden: once my back started to ache, I forgot about how my neck felt.

"What luck!" I said to myself. "Maybe in a few days I'll just be numb. Nothing will hurt. And when the summer is over, I'll go to the hospital for a long vacation."

Pretty soon Gloria pedaled up on her bike. She laid it carefully on the grass.

"Huey couldn't keep up with me, so here I am," she said. "But I can't stay long. My mom is expecting me back."

She stood with her thumbs in the belt loops of her blue jeans, staring at me. Then she whispered, "Julian! Your dad really is doing it? He really is going to make you work all day and all night, all summer long?"

"Only all day," I said.

"He really is *mean,*" Gloria said.

"Well, not exactly," I said. "Actually, I *want* to work. Actually, it was my idea."

"Your idea?" Gloria said.

"Yes. I want to save money. To buy a race car."

"You're going to work all summer? You *want* to?"

"Pretty much," I said.

My forehead was sweaty. I wiped it with the back of my hand. Dirt from the weeds trickled down my neck. I thought, "Of all the not-quite-true things I have ever said, this is the not-quite-truest of all."

"Well," Gloria said, "to each his own."

I didn't know what "to each his own" meant.

Usually I wouldn't ever have asked, because I don't want Gloria to know when I don't already know something. But I was living under emergency conditions. It was too much trouble to pretend I knew everything. I decided that if I wanted to know something, I would just go ahead and ask.

I asked.

"It's something my mother says," Gloria answered. "It means each person has his or her own way of doing things and his or her own things to do. It means if you want to work all summer—it's not for me to say you're crazy. You just might not be crazy. Even though I think you are.

"To each his own," Gloria said again. And she left.

In a little while Huey came up.

"Julian," he said, "may I help you weed?"

"Sure," I said. I wondered why Huey wanted to help.

I have to give him credit. He worked hard. We got the whole garden done before supper.

"Thanks a lot, Huey!" I said when we put the tools away.

"It's nothing," Huey said. "Anyway, Gloria told me I had to help you. She said I should be very kind to you. Because maybe your brain is out of order."

"Oh, really?" I said.

My back was out of order. My neck was out of order. My fingers were out of order. My legs were out of order. On top of that, my best friend was insulting my brain.

"Come on, brain," I said to it. "Lead me to dinner."

And it did. Not only that, it advised me to sneak upstairs and take the sharp rocks out from under Huey's mattress so he wouldn't stop helping me.

6.

The Beginning of Happiness

"Julian!" my mother said. "JULIAN!" she shouted.

My head jerked up. My eyes jumped open like electric-eye doors.

"Julian," my mother said, "if you nod one more time, your chin is going to make a crash-landing in your creamed corn."

"Julian is tired," Huey said.

I was amazed. Huey sounded like he cared. He wasn't sounding like a brother. He was sounding like a friend.

"If you can't eat any more," my mother said, "a nice hot bath might relax your muscles."

"Okay," I said. It sounded wonderful. It sounded like the next best thing to a year in the hospital.

"I'll put lots of bubbles in the water, and I'll get you a nice big clean towel," my mother said. "You just wait till the water's ready."

I listened to the sound of water running into

the tub. Then I ached out of my chair and pained my way to the bathroom.

The bathroom was steamy and full of clouds.

My mother helped me out of my shirt, the way she used to when I was little.

When I got into the tub, she scrubbed my back for me with a washcloth. It felt very good.

"Dad told me he's sorry you're not getting time to learn to ride Gloria's bike," my mom said.

"That's okay," I said. "Of course, I want to learn—but it can wait."

"Also," my mom said, "Dad is very proud of you. He likes the way you stick to what you say you'll do, and the way you work hard. He said you did a very good job with everything."

"He did? He is? Really?" I said.

I started to feel very happy and proud about all the work I was doing. But then I remembered how sore I was. I remembered I didn't feel good; I felt bad.

"Dad is pushing me too hard," I said. "He is making me suffer."

I hoped my mother would say, "I'll get him to let up on you. I'll get him to give you less work."

But she didn't. She just rubbed my neck with the washcloth some more and smiled.

"Sometimes," she said, "suffering is the beginning of happiness."

She helped me out of the bathtub and helped me dry off. When I had my pajamas on, she walked upstairs with me and tucked me in bed, the way she did when I was little.

I wiggled my toes. They ached.

"Suffering isn't happiness!" I said. "Suffering is the opposite of happiness!"

"Yes," my mom said, "but sometimes we all have to suffer a little to do things that are worth doing—to do the things that really make us happy."

"Things like earning money?" I said.

"Yes. Or simple things—like telling the truth," my mother said. "For example, I wonder what you truly think about bicycles."

Usually I wouldn't have told. But I was very tired. If things kept on the way they were, I thought, I'd be the first boy ever to be declared a national disaster.

"You really want to know?" I asked.

"Yes."

"You won't tell anybody? Not even Dad?"

"I won't tell anybody. Not even Dad."

"The truth is—the truth is, I don't like them."

"I thought you didn't like them," my mom said very softly.

I looked at her face. She didn't seem to have a bad opinion of me for not liking bicycles. It did feel good to tell the truth. Once I began to tell the truth, it seemed like it almost had a taste, like some really delicious food to chew on, that I wanted to have more and more of in my mouth.

"I hate bicycles!" I said. "I hate the tubes, the tires, the wheels, the spokes, the pedals, the chain, the fenders, the handlebars, the reflectors, and the lights—and that's just the beginning," I said.

"What's the rest?" my mother said.

"The rest is—I hate the idea of falling."

"You might not fall," my mother said.

"Then again, I might," I said. "That would be suffering."

"Uhm-hmm," my mom said. She smiled again. Then she leaned down and put her arms around me and gave me a hug so big it hurt.

But it felt good, all the same.

7.

I Get My Just Reward

I did a lot of work in the next three weeks.

I cut the lawn and the edges of the grass next to the house.

I swept the garage and washed the garage floor.

I washed my dad's truck, inside and out.

I washed all the downstairs windows of the house.

I scraped old paint off the house where my dad plans to repaint.

Sometimes Gloria and Huey helped me quite a bit. But other times it was bad. It was bad when Gloria came down the street on her bike, ringing her bell or riding one-handed. It was worse when she learned how to ride with no hands. Worst of all were the times when she came by riding Huey on her back fender.

One good thing was that Huey left the sharp rocks on my shelf and didn't put them back under my mattress—even though I wouldn't have known if I'd been sleeping on the tiptoppiest point of Mount Everest.

When I got up on Saturday at the end of the third week, Huey was still sleeping. My mom was shopping, but my dad was still in the kitchen eating breakfast.

"GOOD morning, Julian!" he said very cheerily. "How are you?"

"Alive," I said.

"Excellent!" my dad said. "What could be better?"

I thought it would be better if I were a little more alive than I was. But I didn't say anything; I just sat down at the table.

My dad pushed milk and sugar and toast and jam and oranges and cornflakes toward me.

"Better eat a big breakfast, Julian," he said. "You have a big day in front of you."

As soon as he said that, all the food on the table looked like a new job. I hardly ate anything. Pretty soon I got up from the table.

"So," my father said, "are you ready for a tough day?"

"I'm ready," I said.

"First of all," my dad said, "I hope you're feeling good enough to take some bad news."

"I suppose so," I said.

I thought that after all I had been through, I could take anything.

"Well," my dad said, "this is actually *very* bad news. I think you should sit down before I tell you. So you don't fall down."

"Okay." I sat down.

I still thought I could take anything, but I was afraid he was going to tell me he wanted the entire house rebuilt from the foundation.

"The bad news is—" My dad paused. He started over.

"The horrible news is—" My dad seemed afraid to say it.

"The dreadful news is—" He coughed.

"TELL me!" I demanded.

"Well, the very, very bad news is" —my father was almost whispering—"there are no more jobs. Oh, maybe a few next month. And some next summer. But no more for now. I hope you can stand it."

"I can stand it!" I said. I was ready to head for the door.

"Wait a minute!" my father said. "Today is pay-day!"

He handed me a brown paper bag from the kitchen counter. I opened it. Inside was ten dollars and a book on race cars with lots of pictures and facts about engines and records and high-speed performance.

"Thank you!" I said.

"Just one other thing," my dad said. "Would you mind picking up something in the living room?"

"Glad to," I said. I went to the living room.

"Oh, no!" I said.

Parked next to the couch was a brand-new bicycle, just like Gloria's, except that it was a boy's bike, red with white stripes, and behind the seat on a stick it had a red pennant with my name on it—JULIAN—in big white letters.

"It's a surprise!" my dad said. "I didn't even tell your mother I was getting it for you."

My dad smiled. "You know I don't like it when you make up stories. But after a while I thought the reason that you said you wanted so many jobs was because you didn't want to be around someone with a bicycle. You were afraid you couldn't have your own bicycle. Well, now you have one! Of course, if what you really want is to save money for a race car, you can take it back to the store."

"I don't know," I said. "I don't know what I really want."

I had worked so hard to keep bicycles out of my life. What did I get for it? A bicycle!

I was stunned. I needed to talk to somebody. I needed advice.

"Should I teach you how to ride it?" my dad asked.

"No, thanks," I said. "First I want to show it to Gloria."

8.

I Take Off

I wheeled the red bicycle all the way to Gloria's house. Its silver spokes were shining in the sun as if it was saying "Look at me! Look how beautiful I am!"

"Okay, I'm looking," I said.

Before I could even ring Gloria's doorbell, she came running out.

"I was watching from my window!" she said. "What an excellent bicycle!"

"Yes," I said, "and I want to take it back to the store."

"Take it back to the store!" Gloria said. "What's the matter? Don't you like the color?"

I paused. I was going to say I wanted to trade it in, to have more money saved for a race car. But that wasn't true. And it seemed like I got in a lot of trouble getting out of trouble by saying things I didn't mean.

"Gloria," I said, "I don't *like* bicycles. People fall off bicycles!"

"That's for sure!" Gloria said. "Look!"

She raised the corner of her skirt. Her knee was all scraped up and painted orange.

"I fell yesterday," she said. "A dog ran at me. And to think I've always been afraid of cats, not dogs! We never know what to be afraid of in this life!"

"So you aren't going to ride your bicycle anymore?" I couldn't help asking. Maybe Gloria would stop riding her bicycle. I would take mine back to the store. Things would be just the way they used to be.

"Of course I'm going to ride it. I'm just going to be more careful, that's all."

"But you hurt yourself," I said.

"The fun of it is bigger than the hurting," Gloria said.

She touched the white stripes on my bicycle.

"If you don't like your bike, I'll go with you to return it," she said. "Even if you never ride a bicycle, we'll always be friends. But don't you want to try it?"

I stood for a long time. I remembered how much I used to like my tricycle. But I was too old for tricycles. I thought how I didn't want to do something silly, like smoothing out the street with my nose.

"All right," I finally said. "I'll try it."

"Okay!" Gloria said. "See those two cement

blocks? We'll move them and put the bicycle between them, and then you can get on."

We hauled the blocks into place. I wheeled the bicycle over and got on. It didn't feel so bad.

"Now," Gloria said, "take your feet off the blocks."

I did. At first I kept my balance. Then the bicycle started to lean to one side. I put my feet back on the blocks fast.

"Try balancing a few more times," Gloria said.

I did. It got easier.

"Now use the bike like a scooter," Gloria said.

I moved away from the blocks. Then I skimmed down the driveway, holding on to the handlebar and the bike seat and putting just one foot on the near pedal.

"That was fun!" I said.

"Okay," Gloria said. "Now use the blocks again."

I put the bicycle between the cement blocks and balanced on it again. Gloria took hold of the side of the bicycle seat.

"When your bike leans one way," she said, "steer and lean the other way. Pedal now!" she said. "Take off!"

I pushed the top pedal. I left the blocks behind. Gloria ran beside me, holding the bike seat.

I balanced. I didn't fall—even though every time I pushed the pedal down it seemed like my whole body was dropping into the Grand Canyon.

Gloria let go of the seat.

I turned. I was out on the street. I was heading toward my house.

On the sidewalk I saw Huey.

"Julian! Wow!" he called. He took off toward our house.

I heard Gloria's bicycle bell ring. She pedaled up beside me.

I didn't dare look at her. I was scared I'd fall.

"Keep going!" she shouted. "If you think you're going to fall, just keep pedaling!"

It started to seem like I was standing still. Trees and houses floated by me, like green ships and like white ones.

I saw our big tree with our swing. I saw my mom and dad and Huey standing on the curb.

"Good going!" my mom called.

I saw a pothole. I steered and missed it.

"That's the way, Julian! You've got it!" my dad shouted.

Huey started running along the sidewalk. "There goes my big brother!" he shouted.

We left my house behind. We turned in at the park.

Gloria rang her bell. My flag flapped behind me. We rolled under big trees.

"Isn't it great?" Gloria called. "We can go exploring! We can go on picnics! Isn't it a glorious, glorious summer?"

About the Author

ANN CAMERON writes books in order to "capture the positive energy in life." And her readers, who have followed seven-year-old Julian in and out of trouble since his first appearance in *The Stories Julian Tells*, agree she does just that. Ann Cameron was born in Rice Lake, Wisconsin, attended Radcliffe College and the University of Iowa Writer's Workshop, and now lives in Guatemala. She has known she wanted to be a writer "since about third grade," and is the author of several other books for young readers.

About the Illustrator

DORA LEDER was born and raised in Budapest, Hungary, and came to the United States to study illustration when she was seventeen. She lives in Bucks County, Pennsylvania, in a Victorian farmhouse with five cats, one dog, and her husband.